# The Frog Olympics

First published in 2016 by Wayland
Text © Brian Moses
Illustrations © Wayland Publishers

Wayland
Carmelite House
50 Victoria Embankment
London EC4Y 0DZ

Wayland Australia
Level 17/207 Kent Street
Sydney, NSW 2000

Editor: Victoria Brooker
Designer: Lisa Peacock

A catalogue record for this book is available at the British Library
Dewey number: 823.9'2-dc23

From *The Monster Sale* by Brian Moses published by Frances Lincoln Ltd, copyright ©
2013 Reproduced by permission of Frances Lincoln Ltd

ISBN 978 0 7502 9683 0

Printed in China

3 5 7 9 10 8 6 4

Wayland is a division of Hachette Children's Group,
an Hachette UK Company
www.hachette.co.uk

FSC
www.fsc.org
MIX
Paper from
responsible sources
FSC® C012700

# The Frog Olympics

Written by Brian Moses
Illustrated by Amy Husband

WAYLAND

The news spread quickly,
the word went round,

from lake and ditch,
across boggy ground,

THE FROG OLYMPICS

To garden ponds and further still,
as an audience gathered on the side of a hill,

...for the Frog Olympics.

And frogs of every colour and size,

watched the events through big bulgy eyes.

There were frogs that had swum,
from across the sea...

...there were tree frogs peeping
from every tree...

...at the Frog Olympics.

There were medals for tongues
that could catch most flies…

...and the frog that hopped away with first prize,
was an elderly frog whose tongue when uncurled...

could stretch half-way around the world...

...at the Frog Olympics.

There were medals for winning the three-legged frog,

and for jumping IN

and OUT of a bog.

There was leapfrogging streams
from bank to bank,

…and skilful pole-vaulting over a plank…

...at the Frog Olympics.

Then to celebrate the end of the games,
a torch was lit and they followed the flames...

...to a stream where the final event took place,
a *fast* and *furious* tadpole race...

...at the Frog Olympics.

And, oh, those leaps that were so fantastic,

from frogs that must have had...

...legs of elastic.

While everyone agreed that one day soon,
they might see a frog jumping over the Moon.

(Well, a cow did it once, or so they say, and so frogs keep practising, everyday...)